PEACH BOY

and Other

Japanese Children's Favorite Stories

PEACH BOY

and Other
Japanese Children's Favorite Stories

edited by
Florence Sakade

illustrated by
Yoshisuke Kurosaki

CHARLES E. TUTTLE COMPANY
Rutland, Vermont   *Tokyo, Japan*

Published by the Charles E. Tuttle Company, Inc.
of Rutland, Vermont & Tokyo, Japan
with editorial offices at Suido 1-chome, 2–6, Bunkyo-ku, Tokyo

© *1958 by Charles E. Tuttle Company, Inc.*
All rights reserved

International Standard Book No. 0–8048–0469–9

First edition, 1958
Thirty-ninth printing, 1997

PRINTED IN SINGAPORE

Stories in This Book

Publisher's Foreword

In the autumn of 1953 we published the first edition of *Japanese Children's Favorite Stories from "Silver Bells,"* one of Japan's leading children's magazines. Since then, although the magazine is no longer published, the book has been so popular that successive reprintings have worn the plates past further use, and still orders pour in for it. To meet this continuing demand we have now issued a revised edition of the book with entirely new illustrations and several new stories, in a single volume entitled *Japanese Children's Favorite Stories,* and also in two companion volumes entitled *Peach Boy* and *Little One-Inch.* We are confident these books will meet the same enthusiastic response as did the first edition, and should like to quote the following remarks from the Foreword to that edition:

Parents and teachers all over the world have become increasingly aware of the need to raise their children to be citizens of the world, to become thinking adults who, while proud of their own traditions and heritage, are free of the national prejudices, rivalries, and suspicions that have caused such havoc in the past. To this end they have wanted material that would give their children a sympathetic understanding of the life and culture of other lands. This book will fill some part of this need.

We have chosen those traditional stories that may in a very true sense be called " favorites." They have been loved by the children of Japan for hundreds of years, and have proven no less delightful to Western children, thus showing again that the stories that please the children of one land are likely to please children everywhere.

Each of these stories is to be found in Japan—and often in other countries too—in many forms and versions. We have tried to select the most interesting version in each case and, in our translations, to remain true to the spirit of the Japanese originals. At the same time we have inserted sufficient words of explanation into the text of the stories to make customs and situations that are peculiar to Japan intelligible to Western readers without the need for distracting notes.

Editorial responsibility for the book has been borne by Florence Sakade; both as a mother and as an editor and author of numerous children's publications she has had wide experience in the entertainment and education of children. The English versions are the work of Meredith Weatherby, well-known translator of Japanese literature.

Peach Boy

ONCE upon a time there was an old man and his old wife living in the country in Japan. The old man was a woodcutter. He and his wife were very sad and lonely because they had no children.

One day the old man went into the mountains to cut firewood, and the old woman went to the river to wash some clothes.

No sooner had the old woman begun her washing than she was very surprised to see a big peach come floating down the river. It was the biggest peach she'd ever seen in all her life. She pulled the peach out of the river and decided to take it home and give it to the old man for his supper that night.

Late in the afternoon the old man came home, and the old woman said to him: "Look what a wonderful peach I found for your supper." The old man said it was truly a beautiful peach. He was so hungry that he said: "Let's divide it and eat it right away."

So the old woman brought a big knife from the kitchen and was getting ready to cut the peach in half. But just then there was the sound of a human voice from inside the peach. "Wait! Don't cut me!" said the voice. Suddenly the peach split open, and a beautiful baby boy jumped out of the peach.

The old man and woman were astounded. But the baby said: "Don't be afraid. The God of Heaven saw how lonely you were without any children, so he sent me to be your son."

The old man and woman were very happy, and they took the baby to be their son. Since he was born from a peach, they named him Momotaro, which means Peach Boy. They loved Momotaro very much and raised him to be a fine boy.

When Momotaro was about fifteen years old, he went to his father and said: "Father, you have always been very kind to me. Now I am a big boy and I must do something to help my country. In a distant part of the sea there is an island named Ogre Island. Many wicked ogres live there, and they often come to our land and do bad things like carrying people away and stealing their things. So I'm going to go to Ogre Island and

fight them and bring back the treasure which they have there. Please let me do this."

The old man was surprised to hear this, but he was also very proud of Momotaro for wanting to help other people. So he and the old woman helped Momotaro get ready for his journey to Ogre Island. The old man gave him a sword and armor, and the old woman fixed him a good lunch of millet dumplings. Then Momotaro began his journey, promising his parents that he would come back soon.

Momotaro went walking toward the sea. It was a long way. As he went along he met a spotted dog. The dog growled at Momotaro and was about to bite him, but then Momotaro gave him one of the dumplings. He told the spotted dog that he was going to fight the ogres on Ogre Island. So the dog said he'd go along too and help Momotaro.

Momotaro and the spotted dog kept on walking and soon they met a monkey. The spotted dog and the monkey started to have a fight. But

13

Momotaro explained to the monkey that he and the spotted dog were going to fight the ogres on Ogre Island. Then the monkey asked if he couldn't go with them. So Momotaro gave the monkey a dumpling and let the monkey come with them.

Momotaro and the spotted dog and the monkey kept on walking. Suddenly they met a pheasant. The spotted dog and the monkey and the pheasant were about to start fighting. But when the pheasant heard that Momotaro was going to fight the ogres on Ogre Island, he asked if he could go too. So Momotaro gave the pheasant a dumpling and told him to come along.

So, with Momotaro as their general, the spotted dog and the monkey and the pheasant, who usually hated each other, all became good friends and followed Momotaro faithfully. They walked a long, long way, and finally reached the sea. At the edge of the sea Momotaro built a boat. They all got in the boat and started across the sea toward Ogre Island.

When they came within sight of the island, they could see that the ogres had a very strong fort there. And there were many, many ogres. Some of them were red, some blue, and some black.

First the pheasant flew over the walls of the fort and began to peck at the ogres' heads. They all tried to hit the pheasant with their clubs, but he was very quick and dodged all their blows. And while the ogres weren't looking, the monkey slipped up and opened the gate of the fort. Then Momotaro and the spotted dog rushed into the fort and started fighting the ogres too.

It was a terrible battle! The pheasant pecked at the heads and eyes of the wicked ogres. And the monkey clawed at them. And the spotted dog bit them. And Momotaro cut them with his sword. At last the ogres were

completely defeated. They all bowed down low before Momotaro and promised never to do wicked things again. Then they brought Momotaro all the treasure they had stored in the fort.

It was the most wonderful treasure you can imagine. There was much gold and silver and many precious jewels. There was an invisible coat and hat, and a hammer that made a piece of gold every time you hit it on the ground, and many other wonderful things. Momotaro and his three helpers carried all this in their boat back to the land. Then they made a cart and put all the treasure in the cart and pulled it back to Momotaro's house.

How happy the old man and woman were when they saw their son return safely from Ogre Island! They were very rich now with all the treasure that Momotaro had brought, and they all lived together very, very, happily.

The Magic Teakettle

THERE was once a priest who was very fond of drinking tea. He always made the tea himself and was very fussy about the utensils he used. One day in an old secondhand shop he discovered a beautiful iron kettle used for boiling water when making tea. It was a very old and rusty kettle, but he could see its beauty beneath the rust. So he bought it and took it back to his temple. He polished the kettle until all the rust was gone, and then he called his three young pupils, who lived in the temple.

17

"Just look what a fine kettle I bought today," he said to them. "Now I'll boil some water in it and make us all some delicious tea."

So he put the kettle over a charcoal fire in a brazier, and they all sat around waiting for the water to boil. The kettle started getting hotter and hotter, and suddenly a very strange thing happened: the kettle grew the head of a badger, and a bushy badger tail, and four little badger feet.

"Ouch! it's hot!" cried the kettle. "I'm burning, I'm burning!" And with those words the kettle jumped off the fire and began running around the room on its little badger feet.

The old priest was very surprised, but he didn't want to lose his kettle. "Quick! quick!" he said to his pupils, "don't let it get away. Catch it!"

One boy grabbed up a broom; another, a pair of fire tongs; and the third, a dipper. And away the three of them went, chasing after the kettle. When they finally caught it, the badger head and the bushy badger tail and

the four little badger feet disappeared and it was just an ordinary kettle again.

"This is most strange," said the priest. "It must be a bewitched teakettle. Now, we don't want anything like that around the temple. We must get rid of it."

Just then a junkman came by the temple. So the priest took the kettle out to him and said: "Here's an old iron kettle I'll sell you very cheap, Mr. Junkman. Just give me whatever you think it's worth."

The junkman weighed the kettle on his hand scales and then he bought it from the priest for a very small price. He went home whistling, pleased at having found such a bargain.

That night the junkman went to sleep and all the house was very quiet. Suddenly a voice called: "Mr. Junkman. Oh, Mr. Junkman!"

The junkman opened his eyes. "Who's that calling me?" he said, lighting a candle.

And there he saw the kettle, standing by his pillow, with the badger head, and the bushy badger tail, and the four little badger feet. The junkman was very surprised and said, "Aren't you the kettle I bought from the priest today?"

"Yes, that's me," said the kettle. "But I'm not an ordinary kettle. I'm really a badger in disguise and my name is Bumbuku, which means Good Luck. That mean old priest put me over a fire and burned me, so I ran away from him. But if you'll treat me kindly and feed me well and never put me over a fire, I'll stay with you and help you make your fortune."

"Why, this is very strange," said the junkman. "How can you help me make my fortune?"

"I can do all sorts of wonderful tricks," said the kettle, waving his bushy badger tail. "So all you have to do is put me in a show and sell tickets to the people who want to see me do my tricks."

The junkman thought this was a splendid idea. The very next day he built a little theater out in his yard, and put up a big sign which said: "Bumbuku, The Magic Teakettle of Good Luck, and His Extraordinary Tricks."

Every day more and more people came to see Bumbuku. The junkman would sell tickets out front and then when the theater was full he'd go inside and start beating a drum. Bumbuku would come out and dance and do all sorts of acrobatics. But the trick that pleased people most of all was when Bumbuku would walk across a tight rope, carrying a paper parasol in one hand and a fan in the other. The people thought this most wonderful. They would cheer and cheer for Bumbuku. And after every show the junkman would give Bumbuku some delicious rice-cakes to eat.

The junkman sold so many tickets that he finally became extremely rich. One day he said to Bumbuku: "You must get very tired doing these tricks every day. I now have all the money I need. So why don't I take you back to the temple, where you can live very quietly?"

"Well," said Bumbuku, "I *am* getting a little tired and I *would* like to live quietly in a temple. But that old priest might put me on the fire again, and he might never give me delicious rice-cakes."

"Just leave everything to me," the junkman said.

So the next morning the junkman took Bumbuku and a large amount of money and some of Bumbuku's favorite rice-cakes to the temple.

When they got to the temple the junkman explained to the priest everything that had happened, and he gave all the money to the priest for the temple. Then he said: "So will you please let Bumbuku live here quietly forever, always feeding him rice-cakes like these I've brought and never putting him over the fire?"

23

"Indeed I will," said the priest. "He shall have the honored place in the temple's treasure house. It's really a magic kettle of good luck, and I would never have put it over the fire if only I'd known."

So the priest called his pupils. They put the kettle on a wooden stand, and the rice-cakes on another stand. Then, with the priest carrying one stand, and the junkman carrying the other, and the three pupils following after, they carried Bumbuku carefully to the treasure house, and put the rice-cakes beside him.

It is said that Bumbuku is still there in the treasure house of the temple today, where he is very happy. They still give him delicious rice-cakes to eat every day and never, never put him over a fire. He is peaceful. He is happy.

Monkey-Dance and Sparrow-Dance

ONCE there was an old woodcutter who went so far into the mountains to find wood that he got lost. He walked for a long time, not knowing where he was going, until he suddenly heard music in the distance and smelled the odors of food and drink.

Climbing up to the top of a hill, he saw a great crowd of monkeys. They were eating and dancing and singing, and drinking a kind of wine that they had made from rice. It smelled so good that the old man at once wanted some.

25

They sang and danced beautifully, much to the old man's surprise. Then one monkey took up a bottle made from a gourd, filled it with wine, and said it was time for him to be going home. The other monkeys told him goodbye and he started home. When the old man saw this, he decided to follow the monkey and see if he couldn't get some of the wine for himself.

Before long the gourd-bottle grew very heavy. So the monkey stopped and poured some of the wine into a jar. He hid the gourd with the rest of the wine in the hollow of an old tree, put the jar on his head, and went merrily on his way, balancing the jar carefully.

The old man had been peeping and had seen all this. When the monkey was gone, the old man said: "Surely he won't mind if I just borrow some of that wonderful wine." So he ran to the hollow tree, and filled a jar with some of the wine. "This is wonderful," he thought. "If it tastes as good as it smells, it must be very fine indeed. I'll take this back to my wife—if I can find my way home."

In the meantime his wife was having an adventure too. She was washing clothes under a tree and suddenly noticed that the sparrows were having a kind of party. They too were drinking something that smelled so good the old woman just had to have some.

So, when the sparrows had finished dancing and singing, the old woman quickly tucked one of their gourd-bottles under her robe and hurried home. "I'll take this to my husband," she thought, "for if it tastes as good as it smells, it must be fine indeed."

No sooner had she arrived than her husband appeared, having finally found his way home. "I have something to show you," they both said at the same time. And then, one by one, they told each other their stories. Then they exchanged their bottles and drank the wine.

It tasted delicious, but no sooner had they drunk it than they both felt an uncontrollable desire to dance and sing. The old woman began to chatter and jump around like a monkey, while the old man held his hands out and chirped like a sparrow.

First the old man sang:

> "One hundred sparrows dance in the spring!
> Chirp-a chirp, chirp-a chirp, ching!"

Monkey-Dance and Sparrow-Dance **27**

Then the old lady sang:

"One hundred monkeys making a clatter.
Chatter-chat, chatter-chat, chatter."

They made so much noise that the man who owned the woods they lived in heard them and came running. There he saw the old woman dancing and acting like a monkey, and the old man dancing and acting like a sparrow. "Here, here!" he said. "This will never do. If you're going to dance, a woman's dance should be graceful and lady-like, like a sparrow's dance, and a man's dance should be bold and manly, like a monkey's dance. Not the other way around."

So the old couple stopped dancing and told their landlord the stories of their adventures. "Well, of course," he said, "you've each been drinking the wrong wine. Why don't you change bottles again and see what happens."

After that the old man always drank the monkey wine, and danced in a very manly way. And the old woman always drank the sparrow wine, and danced in a very lady-like way. Everyone who saw them dance and heard their songs thought them very lovely and started imitating them. And that is why to this day a man leaps about nimbly and boldly when he dances, while a woman is much more graceful and bird-like when she dances.

The Long-Nosed Goblins

LONG ago there were two long-nosed goblins who lived in the high mountains of northern Japan. One was a blue goblin and the other was a red goblin. They were both very proud of their noses, which they could extend for many, many leagues across the countryside, and they were always arguing as to which had the most beautiful nose.

One day the blue goblin was resting on top of a mountain when he smelled a very good smell coming from somewhere down on the plains. "My, but something smells good," he said. "Wonder what it is."

So he started extending his nose, letting it grow longer and longer as it followed the good smell. His nose grew so long that it crossed seven mountains, went down into the plains, and finally ended up at a lord's mansion.

Inside the mansion the lord's daughter, Princess White-flower, was having a party. Many other little princesses had come to the party, and Princess White-flower was showing them all her rare and beautiful dress materials. They had opened the treasure house and taken out the wonderful pieces of cloth, all packed in incense. It was the incense that the blue goblin had smelled.

Just at that moment the princess was looking for some place to hang the cloth up so they could see it better. When she caught sight of the blue goblin's nose, she said: "Oh, look, someone's hung a blue pole on the terrace. We'll hang the cloth on it."

So the princess called her maids and they hung the pieces of beautiful cloth on the goblin's nose. The blue goblin, sitting way back on his mountain, felt something tickling his nose, so he began pulling it back in.

When the princesses saw the beautiful pieces of cloth go flying away through the air, they were very surprised. They tried to catch the cloth, but they were too late.

When the blue goblin saw the beautiful cloth hanging on his nose, he was very pleased. He gathered the cloth up and took it home with him. Then he invited the red goblin, who lived on the next mountain, to come and see him.

"Just look what a wonderful nose I have," he said to the red goblin. "It brought me all this wonderful cloth."

The red goblin was jealous when he saw this. He would have turned green with envy except that red goblins can't turn green.

"I'll show you my nose is still the best," the red goblin said. "Just you wait and I'll show you."

After that the red goblin sat up on top of his mountain every day, rubbing his long red nose and sniffing the air. Many days passed and he still hadn't smelled any incense. He became very impatient and said: "Well, I won't wait any longer. I'll send my nose down to the plains anyway, and it's sure to find something good there."

So the red goblin started extending his nose, letting it grow longer and longer, until it crossed seven mountains, down into the plains, and finally ended up at the same lord's mansion.

Just at that moment the lord's son, Prince Valorous, and his little friends were playing in the garden. When Prince Valorous caught sight of the red goblin's nose, he cried, "Just look at this red pole that someone's put here. Let's swing on it."

So they got some thick ropes and tied them onto the red pole and made several swings. Then how they played! Several of the boys would get in the same swing and they'd swing high up toward the sky. They climbed all over the red pole, jumped up and down on it, and one even began to cut his initials in the pole with a knife.

How all this hurt the red goblin, sitting back on his mountain! His nose was so heavy that he couldn't move it. But when the boy started cutting on it, the red goblin pulled with all his might and shook all the boys off his nose. Then he pulled it back to his mountain as fast as he could.

The blue goblin laughed and laughed at the sight. But the red goblin only sat stroking his nose and saying: "This is what I get for being jealous of other people. I'm never going to send my nose down into the plains again."

The Rabbit in the Moon

ONCE the Old-Man-of-the-Moon looked down into a big forest on the earth. He saw a rabbit and a monkey and a fox all living there together in the forest as very good friends.

"Now, I wonder which of them is the kindest," he said to himself. "I think I'll go down and see."

So the old man changed himself into a beggar and came down from the moon to the forest where the three animals were.

"Please help me," he said to them. "I'm very, very hungry."

"Oh! what a poor old beggar!" they said, and then they went hurrying off to find some food for the beggar.

The monkey brought a lot of fruit. And the fox caught a big fish. But the rabbit couldn't find anything at all to bring.

"Oh my! oh my! what shall I do?" the rabbit cried. But just then he got an idea.

"Please, Mr. Monkey," the rabbit said, "you gather some firewood for me. And you, Mr. Fox, please make a big fire with the wood."

They did as the rabbit asked, and when the fire was burning very brightly, the rabbit said to the beggar: "I don't have anything to give you. So I'll put myself in this fire, and then when I'm cooked you can eat me."

The rabbit was about to jump into the fire and cook himself. But just then the beggar suddenly changed himself back into the Old-Man-of-the-Moon.

"You're very kind, Mr. Rabbit," the Old Man said. "But you should never do anything to harm yourself. Since you're the kindest of all, I'll take you home to live with me."

Then the Old-Man-of-the-Moon took the rabbit in his arms and carried him up to the moon. Just look and see! If you look carefully at the moon when it is shining brightly, you can still see the rabbit there where the old man put him so very long ago.

The Tongue-Cut Sparrow

THERE was once an old man who had a very mean wife, with a terrible temper. They didn't have any children, so the old man made a pet out of a tiny sparrow. He took very good care of the little bird, and when he came home from work every day he would pet and talk to it until suppertime, and then feed it with food from his own plate. He treated the sparrow just as if it were his own child.

But the old woman wouldn't ever show any kindness to anyone or anything. She particularly hated the sparrow and was always scolding her husband for keeping such a nuisance around the house. Her temper was particularly bad on wash days, because she very much disliked hard work.

One day while the old man was gone to his work in the fields, the wife was getting ready to wash the clothes. She had made some starch and set it out in a wooden bowl to cool. While her back was turned, the sparrow hopped down onto the edge of the bowl and pecked at some of the starch. Just then the woman turned around and saw what the sparrow was doing. She became so angry that she grabbed up a pair of scissors—and cut the sparrow's tongue right off! Then she threw the sparrow into the air, crying: "Now get away from here, you nasty little bird!" So the poor sparrow went flying away into the woods.

A little while later the old man came home and found the sparrow gone. He looked and looked for his pet, and kept asking his wife about it. She finally told him what she had done. He felt very sorry about it, and the next morning he started out into the forest to look for the sparrow. He kept calling: "Where are you, little sparrow? Where are you, little sparrow?"

Suddenly the sparrow came flying up to the old man. It was all dressed in the kimono of a beautiful woman, and it could speak with a human voice. "Hello, my dear master," the sparrow said. "You must be very tired, so please come to my house and rest."

When the old man heard the sparrow speaking, he knew it must be a fairy sparrow. He followed the sparrow and soon came to a beautiful house in the forest. The sparrow led him into the house and into the parlor. The sparrow had many daughters, and they brought a feast for the old man, giving him many, many wonderful things to eat and drink. Four of the daughters did a beautiful Sparrow Dance. They danced so gracefully that the old man kept clapping and clapping, begging them to keep on dancing.

Before he realized it, the sun began to set. When he saw that it was getting dark he jumped up and said he must hurry home because his wife would be worried about him. The sparrow begged him to stay longer, and he was having such a good time that he hated to leave. But still he said: "No, I really must go."

"Well, then," said the sparrow, "let me give you a gift to take home with you."

The sparrow brought out two baskets, one big and heavy and one small and light. "Please take your choice," the sparrow said.

The old man didn't want to be greedy, so he took the small basket and started for home. When he got home, he told his wife everything that had happened. Then they opened the basket. It was full of all sorts of wonderful things—gold and silver, diamonds and rubies, coral and money bags. There was enough in the basket to make them rich all the rest of their lives.

The old man was very glad when he saw this treasure. But the old woman became very angry. "You fool!" she said. "Why didn't you choose the big basket? Then we would have had much more. I'm going to the sparrow's house myself and get the other basket."

The old man begged her not to be so greedy, saying that they already had enough. But the old woman was determined. She put on her straw sandals and started off.

When she reached the sparrow's house, she spoke very sweetly to the sparrow. The sparrow invited her into the house and gave her some tea

and cookies. When the old woman started to leave, the sparrow again brought out one big basket and one small basket and told the woman to choose one as a gift. The old woman quickly grabbed the big basket. It was so heavy she could hardly get it on her back, but with the sparrow's help she lifted it up and started home.

Along the way the basket got heavier and heavier. The old woman kept wondering what wonderful things were inside the basket. Finally she sat down to rest beside the road, and her curiosity got the better of her. She just had to open the basket! When she did, all sorts of terrible things jumped out at her. There was a devil's head that made frightening noises at her, and a wasp that came flying at her with a long stinger, and snakes and toads and slimy things. How frightened she was!

She jumped up and went running home as fast as she could. She told the old man what had happened. Then she said: "I promise never to be mean or greedy again." And it seems she had actually learned her lesson, because ever after that she was very kind and always helped the old man feed any birds that came flying into their garden.

Silly Saburo

LONG ago there was a boy who lived on a farm in Japan. His name was
Saburo, but he always did such silly things that people called him Silly Saburo.
He could never remember more than one thing at a time, and then would
do that one thing, no matter how silly it might be. His father and mother
were very worried about him, but they hoped he'd get smarter as he grew
older, and they were always very patient with him.

45

One day his father said: "Saburo, please go to the potato patch today and dig up the potatoes. After you've dug them up, spread them out carefully and leave them to dry in the sun."

"I understand," said Saburo. So he put his hoe over his shoulder and went out to the potato patch.

Saburo was busy digging the potatoes when all of a sudden his hoe hit something in the earth. He dug deeper and found a big old pot. When he looked inside the pot he found it was filled with large gold coins. It was a huge treasure that someone had buried there long ago.

"Father said I must first dig things up and then leave them to dry in the sun," Saburo said to himself. So he very carefully spread the gold coins out. Then he went home and said: "I found a pot of gold and spread the gold in the sun to dry."

His parents were very surprised when they heard this. They went running to the potato patch, but someone had taken all the gold. There was

not a single coin left. "Next time you find something," his father said, "you must wrap it up very carefully and bring it home. Now don't forget!"

"I understand," said Saburo. And the next day he found a dead cat in the field. So he wrapped it up very carefully and brought it home, very proud of having remembered.

His father said: "Don't be so silly. When you find something like this, you must throw it in the river."

Next day Saburo dug up a huge tree stump. He thought very hard and remembered what his father had said about the dead cat. So he took the stump and threw it with a great splash in the river.

Just then a neighbor was passing. "You mustn't throw away valuable things like that," the neighbor said. "That stump would have made good firewood. You should have broken it up into small pieces and taken it home."

"I understand," said Saburo, and started on his way home. On his way home he saw a teacup which somebody had left beside the road. "Oh, here's a valuable thing!" said Saburo. So he took his hoe and broke the teapot and teacup up into very small pieces. Then he gathered up the pieces and took them home with him.

"Hello, Mother," he said. "Look what I found and brought home." Then he showed his mother the broken pieces of china.

"Oh, my!" said his mother. "That's the teapot and teacup that I took to your father with his lunch this noon. And you've completely ruined them!"

Next day his parents said: "Everything you do, you do wrong. We'll go out into the fields and work today. You stay home and keep the house." So they left Saburo alone.

"I really don't understand why people call me Silly Saburo," he said to himself. "I do everything just exactly the way people tell me to do."

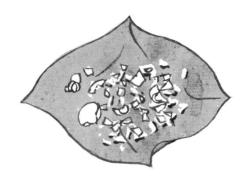

The Toothpick Warriors

ONCE upon a time there was a princess who had a very bad habit. She would lie in bed at night and pick her teeth with a toothpick. That wasn't so bad, but after she was done, instead of throwing the toothpick away as she should have, she would stick it between the straw mats that make the floor of a Japanese house and upon which the princess slept. Now, this was not a very clean habit, and since the princess did this every night the cracks between the mats were soon filled with used toothpicks.

49

One night she was suddenly awakened by the noise of fighting. She heard the voices of warriors and the sound of swords. Frightened, she sat up and lit the lamp beside her bed. She was so surprised by what she saw that she could hardly believe her eyes:

There, right beside her quilts, were many tiny little warriors. Some were fighting, some were singing, some were dancing, and all were making a great deal of noise.

The princess thought that she must be dreaming, so she pinched herself. But, no, she was wide awake, and the tiny warriors were still there making a terrible racket. They made so much noise that she couldn't sleep at all that night, and when she did manage to doze off, she suddenly woke up because it was so quiet. The tiny warriors had left.

She was very afraid, but she was ashamed to tell the lord, her father, because he probably wouldn't have believed her. Yet, next night when she went to bed, the same thing happened again, and the night after that too.

The tiny warriors made so much noise every night that she couldn't sleep, and each day the princess became a little paler than the day before. Soon she became very ill from lack of sleep.

Her father kept asking her what the matter was, and finally she told him. At first he didn't believe her, but finally he decided to see for himself. He told her that she should sleep in his room and he would stand watch in hers.

And so he did. But though he remained awake all night long and watched and waited, the tiny warriors did not come. While waiting, however, he noticed the many toothpicks lying about on the floor. He looked very

carefully at the toothpicks and finally discovered what had been happening.

Next day he called his daughter to him and showed her one of the toothpicks. Its sides were all scarred and cut. The marks were so very tiny that the princess could just barely see them. She asked her father what the marks meant.

Her father explained that the tiny warriors had come to her room because she left toothpicks lying around. They had no swords of their own and wanted some very much. Now, for a tiny warrior, a toothpick made the best possible kind of sword, and that was the reason they came every night.

They hadn't come last night, he said, because he was there with a real sword, and they were afraid. Then he looked at his daughter sternly and asked her why there were so many used toothpicks in her room.

The princess was very ashamed of her bad habit but admitted that she had used the toothpicks and stuck them between the cracks of the mats because she was too lazy to get up and throw them away properly. She also said she was very, very sorry and promised that she would never, never be so lazy again.

Then she picked up all the toothpicks, even those that were at the very bottom of the cracks, and threw them all away. That night the warriors did not come because there were no tiny swords for them. And they never came again.

Soon the princess became healthy again because the warriors no longer kept her awake. She became very neat about everything, and pleased her father greatly by even sweeping the garden every day. She never forgot the tiny warriors, and if she ever used a toothpick again, you may be sure she was very careful to throw it away properly.

The Sticky-Sticky Pine

ONCE there was a woodcutter. He was very poor but very kind. Never would he tear off the living branches of a tree to make firewood. Instead, he would gather only the dead branches on the ground. He knew what happened when you tore a branch off a tree. The sap, which is the blood of a tree, would drip and drip, just as though the poor tree were bleeding. So, since he didn't want to harm the trees, he never tore off the branches.

One day he was walking beneath a high pine tree hunting for firewood when he heard a voice, saying:

> "Sticky, sticky is my sap,
> For my tender twigs are snapped."

The woodcutter looked and, sure enough, someone had broken three limbs off the pine and the sap was running out. Skillfully, he mended them, saying:

> "Now these tender twigs I'll wrap,
> And in that way stop the sap."

And he tore a piece from his own clothes to make a bandage.

No sooner had he finished than many tiny gold and silver things fell from the tree. It was money—a lot of it. The surprised woodcutter was

almost covered up with it. He looked at the tree and smiled and thanked it. Then he took the money home.

There was a great amount and he slowly realized that he was now a very rich woodcutter indeed. Everyone knows that the pine tree is the sign of prosperity in Japan and, sure enough, the grateful pine had made him very rich.

Just then a face appeared in the window. It was the face of another woodcutter. But this woodcutter was neither nice nor kind. In fact, it was he who had torn off the branches of the pine and had broken its twigs. When he saw the money he said: "Where did you get all that money? Look how nice and bright it is."

The good woodcutter held up the money so the other could see. It was oblong in shape, the way money used to be in Japan, and he had five basketfuls. He told the bad woodcutter how he had got the money.

"From that big pine tree?"

"Yes, that was the one."

"Hmm," said the bad woodcutter and ran away as fast as he could go. He ran right up to the old pine tree, and the tree said:

"Sticky, sticky, is my blood.
Touch me, you'll receive a flood."

"Oh, just what I want," said the bad man, "a flood of gold and silver." He reached up and broke off another branch. The pine tree suddenly showered him. But it showered him with sticky, sticky sap—not gold and silver at all.

The bad woodcutter was covered with sap. It got in his hair and on his arms and legs. Since it was so sticky, he couldn't move and though he called for help, no one could hear him. He had to remain there for three days— one day for each branch—until the sap became soft enough for him to drag himself home.

And, after that, he never broke another branch off a living tree.